The Pirate and the Firefly

a boy, a bug, and a lesson in wisdom

Tara McClary Reeves
& Amanda Jenkins

B&H
KIDS

Nashville, Tennessee

On a quiet street, in a peaceful little town, children were walking home from school when suddenly . . .

"Thief!" cried the shopkeeper as Captain Cole burst through the doors, his lunch bag bulging with candy. The scallywag yelled to his pirate friends who were waiting nearby— "Run!"

The boys raced down Mayfair Lane, their feet and hearts pounding. When Mr. O'Bryan was finally out of sight, they stopped to enjoy their stolen treasure.

All except for Oliver.

"What's the problem, me hearty?" Cole asked.

Oliver's head hung low. He murmured, "I, I—I think it's time for me to go home."

Cap'n Cole squeezed the shoulders of his newest recruit. "Aargh! Come on, Ollie. Eat some candy. We be pirates, and this is what pirates do."

Oliver ate the candy, but for some reason it didn't taste as sweet as it usually did. He couldn't stop thinking about poor Mr. O'Bryan, the empty gumdrop bin in the candy shop, and how disappointed his mom would be if she knew what he'd done.

Oliver was so lost in thought that he didn't even notice his firefly friend waiting to welcome him home.

"Mom, do naughty children get cavities?"

"Mom, is stealing ever okay? Like when Daddy steals your covers?"

"Oliver," his mother said softly. "Is something bothering you?"

Oliver swallowed hard. He knew his mom always made him feel better, but he also thought he'd be in trouble if he told her the truth.

"I'm tired," he answered. "Can we talk about it later?"

"Okay," she whispered. "Just remember, I love you and God loves you —all the time. Now get some sleep. Cole's party is tomorrow."

Alone in his room, the darkness matched how Oliver felt in his heart. He was sad and could not sleep. He knew he'd made wrong choices and that his pirate friends didn't feel sorry for what they'd done to Mr. O'Bryan. But he still wanted to be their friend.

He still wanted to be a pirate.

The next day, Oliver's mother dropped him off at the party where his friends were waiting.

"Anchors aweigh!" Cole bellowed. And with that, the little band of buccaneers followed their leader to the backyard.

Oliver had never
seen such a big tree.

Or such an
enormous tree house.

Or a plank so high
off the ground.

As soon as they reached the deck, the captain shouted his next order, "Ollie, ye salty dog! Time to walk the plank!"

Cole moved in closer, pulling out his cardboard cutlass and pointing it at Oliver. "Is ye a scaredy-cat, Ollie?" he teased as the crew began to chant, "O-llie! O-llie! O-llie!"

Oliver stepped out onto the creaky board, his heart thumping wildly in his chest. But before he was forced to go farther, he heard, "Land ho, lads!"

Immediately, the boys obeyed the command and hurried down the ladder. Oliver couldn't get down fast enough.

On the sidewalk in front of her house, Cole's neighbor was strolling with her dolls. In a flash, the nasty pirate overturned the wagon as he and his gang sprinted toward the creek at the end of the street. Oliver glanced over his shoulder to see the little girl in tears. He wanted to go back and help, but he remembered that today he was a pirate.

And he really didn't want to walk that plank.

Cole swung across the rushing water on the rope swing, and the crew followed like they always did. But Oliver let go too soon and landed in the creek. The boys pointed and laughed at him.

"Land lubber!" jeered Cole.

When the pirates returned from their voyage, Oliver was relieved to see his mom's car in the driveway. He was cold and wet and ready to go home.

"Mom, should friends stick together, no matter what?"

"Mom, why are some kids bullies?"

"Mom, is God sad when I break the rules?"

"Mom, if I don't want to be a follower, how do I become a captain?"

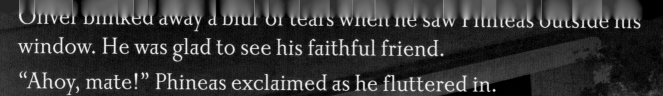

Oliver blinked away a blur of tears when he saw Phineas outside his window. He was glad to see his faithful friend.

"Ahoy, mate!" Phineas exclaimed as he fluttered in.

"Oh, Phineas!" Oliver cried. "I've been a bad, bad pirate! For two whole days, I followed everything Cole did, and none of it was good."

Phineas landed on the Bible next to Oliver's bed.

"Oliver, people who want you to do things that are wrong or dangerous are not true friends. But God wants to be our best friend, and He loves us more than anyone else does. He knows what is right and has given us the Bible to guide us and keep us out of trouble."

"Are you ready for a real adventure, Oliver?"

"Wow!" Oliver exclaimed as Phineas placed a brand new captain's hat on the top of his head.

"Can you imagine what it looks like to follow God instead of a wicked pirate?" Phineas asked. "Psalm 1 begins, *'Oh, the joys of those who do not follow the advice of the wicked, or stand around with sinners, or join in with mockers.'*"

Oliver's imagination set sail. . . .

"We have our heading!" shouted the boys in unison as Oliver and crew made their way back to Mr. O'Bryan's Candy Shop.

It was time to go God's way.

Phineas continued, "Verse two says, *'But they delight in the law of the Lord, meditating on it day and night.'* Oliver, that means God's Word is our treasure. Following His map every day helps us choose what we look at with our eyes, listen to with our ears, touch with our hands, and who we follow with our feet."

Oliver liked imagining himself as a hero instead of a villain. He could hardly wait for his vessel's next turn.

"Thar she blows!" cried Oliver when he saw the little lass still sitting on the sidewalk. "We be back to set things right!"

The crew was happy to be helping instead of pillaging.

"Oliver, feast your eyes on this," Phineas instructed. "Since you've discovered the real treasure of God and His Word, this tree is like your life. Psalm 1:3 says, *'They are like trees planted along the riverbank, bearing fruit each season.'* Oliver, God has given us the Bible so that we can be fruitful and kind and helpful to others. Just look at the smiles on all those faces. You helped put them there."

"And," whispered Phineas as he tucked the covers under Oliver's chin. "I've saved my favorite promise till now, *'God's children will prosper in all they do.'*"

"Good night, wise captain," Phineas said to his young friend. "God's adventure for your tomorrow is already mapped out."

Oh, the joys of those who do not follow the advice of the wicked, or stand around with sinners, or join in with mockers. But they delight in the law of the LORD, meditating on it day and night. They are like trees planted along the riverbank, bearing fruit each season. Their leaves never wither, and they prosper in all they do.

—Psalm 1:1–3